Sylvie Kantorovitz

To Sam, who started out very tiny.

To Doctor W. Bruce Clark.

To the whole NICU team at Albany Medical Center.

 and to Flora Tikva.

Published by Charlesbridge • 85 Main Street • Watertown, MA 02472
(617) 926-0329 • www.charlesbridge.com

Library of Congress Cataloging-in-Publication Data
Kantorovitz, Sylvie.
The very tiny baby / Sylvie Kantorovitz.
p. cm.
Summary: A very young boy tells his teddy bear about his mixed feelings over the premature birth
of his new sibling, and his guilty resentment at the adults' preoccupation with the tiny baby.
ISBN 978-1-58089-445-6 (reinforced for library use)
ISBN 978-1-60734-635-7 (ebook)
1. Premature infants—Juvenile fiction. 2. Teddy bears—Juvenile fiction.
3. Jealousy in children—Juvenile fiction. 4. Ambivalence—Juvenile fiction.[1. Premature babies—Fiction.
2. Babies—Fiction. 3. Sibling rivalry—Fiction. 4. Teddy bears—Fiction.] I. Title.
PZ7.K1284Ver 2014
813.54—dc23   2012038697
Printed in Singapore
(hc) 10 9 8 7 6 5 4 3 2 1

Illustrations and hand lettering done with micron pens, colored pencils, and gouache on Canson paper
Text type set in Bodoni
Color separations by KHL Chroma Graphics, Singapore
Printed and bound September 2013 by Imago in Singapore
Production supervision by Brian G. Walker
Designed by Susan Mallory Sherman

Bob

me, Jacob

There is a baby growing
in my mommy's belly.

my mommy

the baby in
her belly

When I put my ear on my mommy's belly,
I can hear noises. I can also feel some
kicking.

It is weird!

My mommy is happy about the baby.

My daddy is happy about the baby.

I am not sure if I am
happy about the baby.

Mommy says
when the baby is
old enough,
we can play together.

Daddy says one day
we will all have
ice cream together.

Grandma says
a brother
or a sister
can become
a best friend.

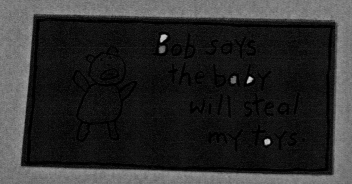

Bob says
the baby
will steal
my toys.

Something bad happened.

The baby is coming out too soon.

Daddy took Mommy to the hospital.

Mommy was scared.

Daddy was scared.

Grandma came over.

Grandma is scared too.

Grown-ups can be scared.

I didn't know.

Grandma explained things to me.

Babies need to stay inside their mommies for 9 months.

This way they get big and strong.

Babies should not come out too soon.

Babies who come out too soon are called preemies.

Preemies can get very sick.

Grandma says no, we cannot put the baby back.

At the hospital, there are machines to help preemies get stronger.

Grandma says I will **not** get sick too.

Is the baby going to die?

Grandma didn't know.

It is lonely at home.

Since the doctor is with the baby, Mommy and Daddy should be here **with me!**

Grandma reads to me.

But she is not paying attention.

Even when Mommy and Daddy are home, they are not paying attention either.

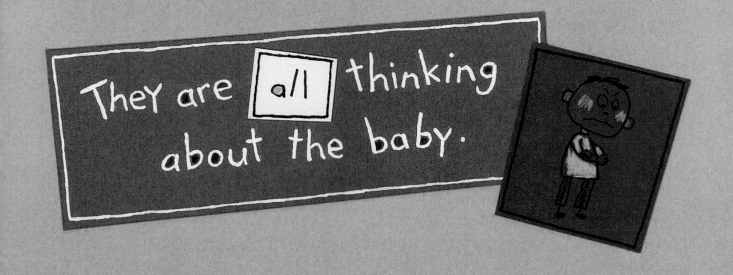

They are all thinking about the baby.

I am thinking about the baby too.

I am thinking mean thoughts.

I think the baby is ruining my life.

I think we should give the baby away.

I wish
the baby
would
die.

Mommy says, Good news!
The baby is going to be OK.

Mommy is smiling again.

Daddy is singing again. ♪ ♫

Grandma is paying attention again.

But the baby is not coming home yet.

The baby is not strong enough to nurse.

Mommy uses a machine.

woosh woosh woosh

The machine pumps Mommy's breast and the milk comes out into a little bottle.

The breast pump is very **loud**.

Every day Mommy takes the milk to the hospital in a little cooler.

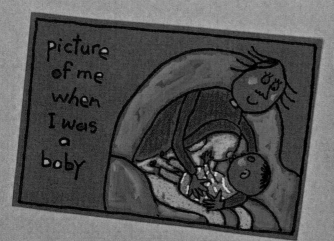

picture of me when I was a baby

I am a big boy now. I do not nurse anymore.

Daddy is taking me to see the baby today.

At the hospital, we take the elevator
to the very top floor.

Before we see the baby, we have to scrub our hands with special little brushes and lots of soap.

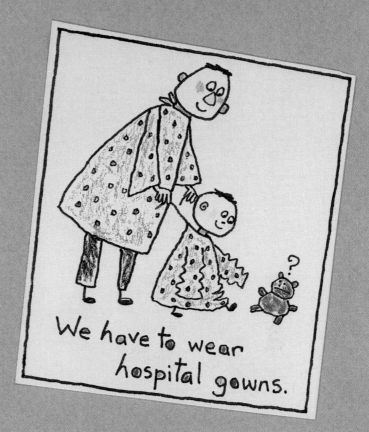

We have to wear hospital gowns.

We need to keep our germs away from the preemies. Preemies are so little that even friendly germs can make them sick.

friendly germs

a mean germ

The baby is in a special box
called an incubator.

When Linda needs
to go home,
Darlene comes.

And when Darlene
goes home, Josh comes.

Sometimes preemies forget to breathe.
The alarm rings and
the nurse nudges the baby.
Then the baby breathes again.

Big people
like me
do not forget
to breathe.

The baby is
really small.

Smaller than Bob, even.

The baby doesn't do anything interesting.

Out of the incubator, the baby wears a tiny hat to stay warm.

Sometimes the baby stretches.

It looks a bit like a frog.

Mostly the baby sleeps.

It is very boring.

Mommy is in love with the baby.

I can tell.

They all love the baby.

I am happy
the baby is well.

I want to be the only one again.

Bob is sick of the baby.

Me too.

Grrrrrrr

This is how I feel inside sometimes.

I can be a cute baby again.

But Mommy says
she doesn't **want**
2 babies.

Mommy wants her Jacob
to be a special big brother.

Daddy says
when the baby
comes home,
he will need
my big-boy
help.

I guess Mommy and Daddy love me too.

I forgive them for forgetting to love me.

After all, that baby took them by surprise.

The baby is coming home today!

I can't wait.

Bob is still a little bit worried.

Here they come! Here they come!

Wow! So tiny still.

Hello, tiny baby.